P9-CAN-835

Weekly Reader Children's Book Club presents

THE LUCK OF
HARRY WEAVER

WEEKLY READER
CHILDREN'S BOOK CLUB

FRANKLIN WATTS, INC.

845 Third Avenue
New York, N.Y. 10022

THE LUCK OF
HARRY
WEAVER

by Mildred Wilds Willard

illustrated by Charles Robinson

For my son,
*   John Michael Willard*

SBN 531-01967-5

Copyright © 1971 by Mildred Wilds Willard
Library of Congress Catalog Card Number: 72-131147
Printed in the United States of America
Weekly Reader Children's Book Club Edition

CONTENTS

1
A GOOD VISITOR

Harry Weaver decided, after sad experience, that a school bus was always late if there was a dust-swirling wind, pouring rain, or a blow-in-your-face snow. Today it was windy, and so, of course, the bus was late. Then this same contrary bus was extra early on those mornings when he dawdled, mislaid his boots, or spilled jelly down the front of his shirt.

Being at the mercy of a wheezing, unpredictable school bus was one big reason why Harry was sorry his mom had ever found her "dream house" way out here in Green Hill Acres.

Harry couldn't see much of a green hill

anyplace in this new subdivision. It was mostly mud tracks and bare skeletons of being-built houses in a flat area that used to be a cornfield. A big billboard at the entrance to the whole plot said, "HALF-ACRE HOME SITES—A RESTFUL COMMUNITY OF THREE- AND FOUR-BEDROOM HOMES WITH FAMILY-SIZE CLOSETS."

So for this Harry had left his best friends at Oak Street School in his old city neighborhood and had started fourth grade last September among strangers. Now here it was after school and here was Mary Marshall, as usual minding his business and telling him what he should and shouldn't do. (Words failed Harry when he tried to describe Mary Marshall to his parents.) Standing in front of the school, he clapped his hands over his ears, but he could hear her calling him names anyhow.

"You're nothing but a wisher, Harry Weaver," Mary chanted. "You're a do-nothing, pay-no-attention, wishy-washy wisher, and I wish I'd never picked you for our homeroom keep-the-blackboard-clean committee, and I won't ever pick you again!"

Harry hurried away from her, calling back, "So, see if I care." Then he ran out of hearing distance around the corner of the building. From there he could see when the bus pulled up at the corner to take him on his homeward trip.

As he peeked around to check on the bus, he saw a skinny seventh-grade girl, wearing the badge and cap of a bus-stop guard. She was talking to some of the girls in his room. Whatever she told them made them squeal. At once they ran across the playground toward the gym building.

Why did they run off like that? Harry wondered. They all took the same bus he did. And where were all the others in his room who usually were waiting with him?

When Harry came out of hiding from around the corner of the building, the bus-stop guard scowled at him and asked, "Aren't you one of the fourth graders who take Bus Two? How come you're standing here?"

"Where would I be standing?" said Harry. "This is where my bus loads."

"Oh, good night!" she shrieked. "Are all you little kids deaf? I came to your room and read off the notice myself. This afternoon your bus loads in front of the gym."

Harry made a dash across the playground for the faraway section of the sprawling school building. He got there just in time to see his bus turning onto the main highway a block away. He started to run after it but gave up. Now he would have to walk home, all those long, dismal, muddy miles. Hitchhiking was strictly forbidden, both at home and at school. With his continuous and everlasting bad luck, Harry knew he'd never dare try to break a rule.

And it wouldn't do any good to call his mom. This happened to be the afternoon she was driving to the airport to meet his cousin, Petty Officer Third Class James Harold Weaver. She said she'd leave the key in the mailbox because Harry would probably make it home before she did. Fat chance of that now.

Harry couldn't wait to see Jim again. In fact, he'd been feeling happy for once in a long time, before he took all that name-calling from Mary and then missed the bus. Jim should have some exciting tales to tell, after being away at sea and in ports like Hong Kong and Tokyo, Japan, and other places that Harry couldn't spell or pronounce.

"I'm going to join the Navy the minute they'll take me," mumbled Harry to no one because there was no one around.

When he looked back at the school, Buses Three and Four were pulling away from the front of the gym where he should have been standing. But he couldn't get home by taking either of them anyway. They went in other directions, to places like Pepper Tree Farms Estates, to Countryside, and to Kensington Garden homes.

That was the trouble with this new school. And it was why he couldn't make friends. Everyone was scattered all over, and they'd already become friends before Harry got there. Anyhow, it seemed that the worst kids in the school for teasing other people all took the same bus that he did.

Harry could list many other reasons why

this new school was nothing but trouble and misery. He was sure that he'd never get a fair chance in a place like this because his name started with W, and his teacher, Miss Olson, seated everyone according to the alphabet. This put him at the very last desk in the very last row.

At his other school, the teacher let the students pick the places where they wanted to sit. Harry liked to be up front. Then no one bothered him, and if ever he didn't pay attention, the teacher could tap him on the shoulder and say, "Are you with us, Harry Weaver?"

In this place, in his lonely back seat, he just stared out of the window and felt gloomy and grumpy. There was nothing much to look at in the big vacant field beyond the stretch of school lawn, so after awhile he got to playing a game all to himself. He tried to make out what kind of cars were passing by on busy County Line Road. He kept score by the day and by the week to see if there were more Fords, Chevrolets, Volkswagons, or whatever. Maybe someday he could send in a report of his scores to the presidents of these auto companies and they'd give him a job and then he could quit school for good.

Lately his bad luck had been unusually bad. Mary Marshall couldn't seem to let him alone. She saw his score count of passing cars in his notebook and tattled to the teacher. Then a show-off kid by the name of Eddie Beckman, who sat up front because he had B for an initial, answered all the questions that Miss Olson asked Harry. How could he have a chance with an eager-beaver kid like that sitting in front of him, and so close to the teacher?

Harry was forever thinking up some things he could do to get even with Eddie Beckman. In yesterday's arithmetic study period, he printed a sign that said, "I LOVE ME," and he was going to pin it on Eddie's back when class was over. Mary Marshall saw him and told the teacher.

It helped, as he trudged along the side of the highway, to think of more and better tricks to play on Eddie. For a while Harry

kicked a stone along until it went slithering across the road in front of a truck. His arms ached from carrying his lunch box, as well as his social studies book, his speller, and arithmetic exercise book. The teacher had made him bring all these home.

By the time he could see the billboard up ahead that marked the entrance to Green Hill Acres, Harry was hot and tired. Then he heard a horn honking, and a car pulled up beside him and stopped.

"Hi, there, fella!" a cheery voice called. Harry recognized his cousin Jim leaning out of the car window.

Harry climbed into the back seat while his mom complained, "Where have you been? I drove down to school when I didn't find you at home. Your teacher said you'd left with the others."

"I missed the bus," said Harry. "It loaded in a new place, and everyone was too mean to tell me."

"Or didn't you bother to listen when you *were* told?" his mother said.

Jim laughed and said, "Everyone has some bad luck now and then."

"But I've had it every minute of every day since we moved here," Harry grumbled.

His mom didn't bother to explain any of the painful details to Jim. Instead, she told Harry about all the exciting places that Jim had said he'd seen since he was at their house last time. Harry looked at his grown-up, seafaring cousin with new awe and interest. Jim was on his way home to Middletown, Ohio, where he would spend a couple of weeks' leave. A leave was what they called a vacation in the Navy.

When his mom bumped into the driveway, which hadn't been paved yet, she suggested that Harry carry Jim's seabag into the house and to the guest bedroom. But Jim toured all through the place first, and at every turn, he exclaimed, "What are you beefing about, Harry? This beats the Navy, and it's a lot nicer than where you used to live." In Harry's bedroom—decorated in red, white, and blue—Jim stretched out on the bed and said, "You didn't have a room like this back in your old place. How come you don't like it here?"

"I hate the kids who go to my school," said Harry. "It's been awful getting teased at the bus stop."

Jim jumped up from the bed and grabbed his seabag. "Wait a minute!" he said. "I've got a powerful magic maker that I brought all the way from Hong Kong. This little guy can make wishes come true so fast that you've got to be careful of what you're wishing."

Harry stared at the seabag. What kind of magic maker could come out of this tightly packed roll of clothes? But before he could ask, Jim brought out a small round jar which he said was a cage. He handed it to Harry and told him to look at the tiny flowers and birds painted on it.

"That's hand-painted," said Jim, "on account of it's used for such a special purpose."

"What kind of purpose?" asked Harry, as Jim took the lid off the jar.

"Because it's home for a very special extraordinary guy named Mr. Chang," Jim replied. "What a character!"

The "character" Harry saw inside the cage was only a fat black bug about an inch long, sitting stiff and still as though he were stuffed. "Is it dead?" asked Harry. "Or is it a fake?"

"There's nothing dead or fake about this fellow," said Jim. "You should see him in action. He's a famous champion Chinese fighting cricket. Just wait until I tickle him with the rat's whisker I have with me."

Jim touched the cricket's threadlike black legs gently with the silvery sliver that he called a rat's whisker. The insect came to sudden life, moving its many legs in violent sweeps, and it waved the long antennae curling from its head.

"See, he's plenty mad now," said Jim. "He's ready to fight whoever's just bothered him. If we were to put another cricket in front of him right now, Mr. Chang would really go after him."

"Where'd you get such a thing?" Harry asked.

"That's a long story," said Jim. "A friend of mine got him in Hong Kong for saving a man's boy from drowning. This cricket is the son of the son of a famous cricket fighter named Genghis Khan. I've watched him win a battle. He's terrific."

"Gee!" said Harry. "I've never seen a cricket fight. I never knew they had fights."

Jim described the one such event he had seen, which he said was a very popular sport among the Chinese. "This cricket named Genghis Khan was supposed to have brought in about a hundred thousand dollars in a single fight. The Chinese believe that the fighting spirits inside these tiny champs get passed on to other crickets hatched out of eggs near the graves of the dead fighters."

"How do they know where these cricket graves are?" asked Harry. He had a feeling that Jim was making up this wild tale just to make him feel better.

"They know," said Jim. "The Chinese

treat these fighting champs just like they treat their famous army generals. When the champs die of old age, or accidentally, their owners buy them silver coffins and have a burial service. They believe crickets bring them good luck, so they keep them in these fancy cages by their hearths at home."

"How do you know this one's a lucky charm?" Harry asked. He'd heard about geese that could lay golden eggs, and other stories of good luck and good wishes come true, but he'd never heard about Chinese crickets with the spirits of dead cricket warriors inside them.

"I tried him out," said Jim. "I didn't believe in him either. So I wished that my leave would be okayed to come back to the states, and it came through the very next day. Then some guy who'd borrowed ten bucks from me paid it back just ten minutes after I wished he would. And a girl I knew back in Middletown wrote me a long letter, just about the time I was wishing I knew what had happened to her."

Jim closed the cricket cage with the little magic maker inside and handed it to Harry. "Why don't you take him and try him out?" he said.

"You mean I should start wishing for things I want?" asked Harry.

"Sure, why not," Jim told him. "But be careful. Don't wish you're fifteen feet tall or something crazy like that, or it'll happen."

"Aw, this little bug couldn't make me stretch that tall," said Harry. "But maybe I'll wish away my red hair so the girls will quit teasing me." Harry also had a round face with pink apple cheeks and freckles.

Right away Jim warned him, "Don't wish your hair away or in a half a second you'll start getting bald. I'm not kidding you. This lucky cricket's as magic as they come."

"Then I'll try him on something easier," said Harry. He held his hands over the clay cage, shut his eyes, and said, "I'd like Mom to have chocolate cake with chocolate icing for dinner."

At the very moment Harry opened his

eyes, there was his mother standing in the doorway. "What's going on?" she said. "It's been a long time, Jim, since your last trip here. But I hope I remembered your favorite dessert. Wasn't it chocolate cake? I baked one this afternoon especially for you."

"It sure is my favorite, Aunt Martha," said Jim.

Harry gasped in surprise. Quickly he took the lid off the cage and peered inside at the magic, wish-granting cricket that truly did have the spirits of many brave ancestors inside his tough, glistening black body.

"I'm glad I didn't wish I was fifteen feet tall or something as crazy as that," he said.

Jim just nodded, knowing all the time that the chocolate cake wish was safer.

2
PROOF AND A BUS RIDE

Harry was relieved that his mother didn't seem to mind a champion fighter cricket around the house. When Jim told her that Mr. Chang was a magic maker, she smiled and said, "Good for him. I've got a whole bundle of wishes. I wish that Harry's report card would improve, and that he'd get up early enough to eat his breakfast and get to the bus stop on time. I wish he'd make some new friends here, instead of pining away for his old ones. I wish he'd quit hating girls in his school who only try to help."

At that point Harry had run off to get

some food for his new pet. Jim said he could chop up a piece of lettuce leaf. According to Jim, the Chinese fed their pet crickets boiled chestnuts, lotus seeds, and ground mosquitoes mixed with rice. But Harry didn't think his mother had any of those things around the house.

Jim also told Harry that if Mr. Chang got sick from eating too much, he should be fed red ants. If he caught a cold, chopped mosquitoes were good, and in the summer Mr. Chang could be cooled off with a special dish of green pea shoots.

The next day, which was Saturday, Harry went with his parents to drive his cousin to O'Hare Airport in Chicago. On the way, Jim entertained them with more stories of the champion fighting cricket.

"I've looked at Mr. Chang very closely," Jim said. "One of his wings has notched edges like the teeth of a tiny saw. He makes that *treee-eeet creee-eeet* sound by drawing one wing across the other, like a violinist. And did you know that the lady cricket has sound receivers just below her front knee joints? If she likes the music she hears the male cricket play, she comes to share his home, which is a hole in the ground."

"Well, that's one way of picking a husband," said Mr. Weaver.

If Harry had any doubts about Mr. Chang's magic-making ability before, he was really convinced after the trip to the airport. Harry had brought Mr. Chang along in his cage, which was stuffed in his jacket pocket.

Mr. Weaver said that they might not be able to see Jim's plane take off if they couldn't find a parking space at the busy airport. As they entered the parking lot, Harry looked up and down the double rows of parked cars. Then he saw a puff of smoke from an auto exhaust far up the line.

"Look, Dad," Harry shrieked. "Isn't that someone getting ready to pull out way up there?"

"Where?" cried Mr. Weaver. "You're right, Harry. What a break!"

"This is our lucky day," said Mrs. Weaver, when they pulled into the vacated space.

But Harry patted his cricket cage and said, "Thanks, Mr. Chang." Then he said to Jim, "Guess who got us that parking place?"

"You did," said Jim. "You were the one who noticed the motor running on that car. You've got good eyesight."

"No, it was really Mr. Chang," said Harry. "I gave him a hard brain-wave thought, and just like that he made it happen." Harry snapped his fingers to show how fast the magic had taken place.

Jim just nodded and smiled.

On the Monday morning after Jim had gone, Harry didn't have time to dislike getting up. Mr. Chang woke him with some cheerful chirping. By the time his mom came yawning into the kitchen to start breakfast, Harry was already there and dressed for school. He was busily squashing a lettuce leaf for Mr. Chang.

"What a shock!" cried Mrs. Weaver. "I didn't even call you once."

"Mr. Chang woke me," said Harry.

"Good for him!" Mrs. Weaver said. "If he performs no more magic than that, it's enough for me, and he's very much worth his room and board."

Because Harry had gotten dressed so early, he had time to eat a bowl of oatmeal and a soft-boiled egg on toast. He also did some thinking about where Mr. Chang should spend the day. Harry certainly needed some magic-making in school, and it would be easier for Mr. Chang to be right there with him. But where could he keep a valuable champion in a roomful of prying eyes, pinchy fingers, and pushy tattletales?

His schoolroom desk was small and too full already. Besides, Monday morning was desk inspection. Eddie Beckman was desk inspector because he sat in a front seat, and wouldn't he like to tell about a cricket cage in Harry's desk!

Well, maybe he should wear his boots. After he got to school, he could transfer the cage from his pocket to the toe of one boot. It

would be a good place for Mr. Chang to rest.
He'd think he was in a dark hole in the
ground and he could get air. Boots were kept
on the floor in the back of the room, under
the hat and coat hooks. Harry could keep his
within reach of his back seat.

When he was pulling on his boots, his
mother gave him a smile of surprise. "What a
pleasant sight," she exclaimed. "I didn't even
have to remind you this morning, and it does
look like rain."

Harry had so much time that he didn't
have to run to the bus stop. When he got
there, Chuck Moller, a big bully of a sixth-
grade boy, was the only one waiting. Harry
braced himself to hear Chuck's usual teasing
about his "noisy" boots, but Chuck made a
kind of friendly half salute with his hand and
said, "Hiya, Harry! Let's guess who'll show up
next."

Harry guessed with a name or two, but he
didn't care who came next. He glanced down
at his feet, wondering if he really had put on
his boots. Then he realized why Chuck hadn't

teased him about them. The boots were buck-led shut for once and were covered up by the legs of his pants. Chuck never noticed Harry was wearing them. And as the others arrived, they didn't notice either.

Later on, just before the bus came, Barbie Myers was the one to get a dose of teasing. It had begun to rain and her umbrella blew in-side out when she came running to catch the bus. This time she was the one who slipped in a mud puddle, but she didn't fall down com-pletely like Harry usually did. That was be-cause Harry reached out and caught her.

When they had all pushed each other on board the bus and were rolling on their way, everyone seemed unusually quiet. Maybe they all felt sleepy, as Harry did, after an exciting weekend.

It had started to rain harder, and Harry was watching the pattern-making of the rivu-lets against the steamy bus window when he heard a sudden, very loud *"treee-eeet."* He clapped his hand over the bulge in his jacket pocket and held his breath. Why didn't the girls up front start to giggle about something? But no one did anything noisy enough to drown out the repeated chirping.

At last there was silence and Harry took a breath of relief. Maybe Mr. Chang had gone back to sleep. But no. He was wide-awake and felt like announcing his presence once again. This time it was louder, a double *"treee-eeet"* and *"creee-eeet."*

Bill Bassett turned around in his seat directly in front of Harry and called to everyone behind them, "Hey, you guys, did you hear that? It sounded like some kind of chirping bug."

"What kind of bug?" asked Chuck Moller. "Let's see if we can find it. Mr. Swanson wants everyone in school to bring all the insects they can find to the science lab. He pins them on a specimen board for the junior-high study project."

Chuck pulled himself out of his seat and lurched up and down the bus aisle, looking on the floor and telling everyone to move a big foot. Bill followed along, rechecking under the same feet. When they were both close to Harry, Mr. Chang chose that moment to trill out another happy *"creee-eeet,"* and Bill yelled, "It's here someplace and it sounds like a cricket."

"You mean to say a cricket got on our bus without a ticket!" cried Chuck.

Like a chorus, a couple of others repeated his singsong rhyme. "A cricket without a ticket, a cricket without a ticket."

"Everyone help find it," called Bill.

Harry stayed stiff as stone. If he didn't move and didn't breathe, maybe Mr. Chang would realize his own danger and keep quiet.

3

THE CHARM OF
MR. CHANG

This lucky cricket felt too sure of himself to keep silent. Bill Bassett crawled around searching for it. "That bug must be here someplace," he said. "I think it's inside Harry Weaver's lunch box. Maybe it's eating his sandwich."

The others laughed at this, and while they laughed, Harry had his good idea, as though someone was magically handing it to him. He became actor extraordinary to turn their attention from him. He stood up, stared at the floor in front of the bus, and then gave out a squeal of happy discovery.

"There it is!" he cried. "It's jumping up there right this minute by Helen Peters' foot!"

Both Bill and Chuck rushed to look at the spot where Harry was pointing. But Helen had also heard his announcement. She scrambled to a kneeling position on her seat and squealed.

"Get that bug off me," she yelled.

Her flinging arms jostled the hunched-over back of the bus driver as he peered through the steam-clouded, rain-streaked windshield. At once he pulled to the side of the road and stopped. He pulled on the hand brakes with a loud grunt, stood up, and faced his noisy, excited passengers.

"Sit down!" he commanded. "Every one of you! Sit down!"

Helen Peters tried to explain. "There was this big, black, ugly-looking cricket that I saw. Then it crawled on my leg and bit me," she said.

Chuck Moller agreed. "Sure—and I saw it, too. We tried to catch it 'cause our science teacher told us to bring him all the insects we could find."

Again the bus driver demanded quiet. "There's lots of insects in that field next to your school," he said. "So you all sit down and wait until we get there before you move again. Driving's bad enough in this rain."

That warning made everyone sit down. The command of the bus driver had silenced even Mr. Chang. For a while after that crucial moment, they drove on silently, while most of them looked down at the floor to make sure a big black cricket wasn't nibbling on their legs. Helen stayed kneeling on the seat.

Finally, after one more stop to pick up additional riders, the bus driver delivered them all to the front door of the school building.

Once inside, Harry had to face the problem created by bringing Mr. Chang to school. If his chirping had raised such a commotion on the bus, what would happen when he decided to make music in the middle of arithmetic?

When Harry got to his back corner seat, he pulled off his boots. After removing the cage and Mr. Chang from his pocket, he stuffed them down into the toe of one boot and then started worrying. What if the boot got kicked by some careless kid grabbing for a coat or hat on the hooks above?

As Harry looked around, he noticed that the window nearest him had a wide ledge on the outside. The rain had stopped, so he opened the window far enough to stick out his head. The outside ledge continued on back to connect with a vertical column on the building. This made a protected corner within easy reach, and it would be completely out of sight.

Before anyone could notice what he was doing, he got the cricket cage from his boot and reached out to place it in this safe corner. All day Mr. Chang could breathe in fresh air through the holes in his cage, and his happy chirps would be heard only by the insects in the vacant field beyond.

After class started, Harry kept thinking about Mr. Chang, and now and then he

glanced at the window, wondering if there was a wind. But no branches were blowing and the sun was trying to shine. During arithmetic class, all eyes turned to the blackboard on the other side of the room, and Harry tried to forget about Mr. Chang and pay attention.

The teacher asked Harry to work a problem on the blackboard and he got it right.

"Very good," said Miss Olson. "You see how easy it is when you really try."

Harry turned to the window to send out a thank-you thought wave to the magical Mr. Chang. Then his attention froze to one spot and his heart stopped. Something small and very black was sitting on the *inside* of the windowsill. He blinked to see better. Maybe it was only a black spot in front of his eyes from trying to concentrate so hard on arithmetic.

Then the black spot moved. It hopped again, and it hopped closer to him. Then it hopped back and stood at the open window, studying the inviting field and freedom. Both long black antennae waved as it poised for its leap.

Harry stood up and made a quick grab. He was able to catch the cricket, and now he held it gently enclosed in his hot hand, hoping he hadn't pressed too hard on its legs or wings. However, the teacher saw him and said, "Take the insect you just caught to the window, Harry, and let it go."

By now the whole class had turned around, and her words hit him like an icicle.

"Did you hear me, Harry?" Miss Olson said. "Don't just stand there staring. I will not have anyone teasing the girls with an insect."

"But this isn't what you think, and I wouldn't—" Harry managed to say.

"Do what I said, please," insisted Miss Olson.

Again Harry tried to explain, but his tongue tied and his jaws locked.

Then Mary Marshall waved her hand. "Couldn't Harry take the insect he caught to Mr. Swanson?" she said. "We're supposed to collect all kinds of bug specimens for him. He's got an honor roll and we get our names printed on it if we make a good contribution."

"Thank you, Mary, for reminding me of Mr. Swanson's request," said Miss Olson. "You may take it to him, Harry. But after this do your insect-catching outside of arithmetic class."

Harry winced. He knew that if he ever heard the voice of doom it would surely sound like Mary Marshall's. However, he could do nothing else but get out of the classroom. Somehow he'd find a safe place to keep his cricket until he could get the cage off the outside window ledge.

Harry walked quickly toward the door with the insect in his closed fist. Then Eddie Beckman jumped out of his front seat and held up a small glass bottle. "Put your bug in here, Harry," he said. "If you don't, you might smother it. I saved this bottle from the time I took pills for my allergy. I just punched some holes in the lid with the point of my compass."

Gratefully Harry reached for the bottle. He let the cricket fall into it and went on his way. However, Eddie Beckman soon came trailing close behind him.

Out in the hall, Eddie snatched back his

bottle and said, "Miss Olson said I could go, too, so I get to give this specimen to Mr. Swanson. It's my bottle."

"It's my cricket," cried Harry. "You give that to me or I'll—"

Eddie refused, and Harry made a grab for it. Eddie stuck it in his pocket and started for the stairs which led to the science lab. Then Harry stuck out his foot and managed to trip him. He wrestled with Eddie until he could pry the bottle away from him. Just then a firm hand grabbed his arm and jerked him up. Harry stood facing a frowning Mr. O'Brien, the principal, who demanded, "Give me some explanation, please, for such conduct."

Eddie promptly reported, "Harry tripped me. Miss Olson gave us permission to take this cricket specimen to Mr. Swanson but it's my pill bottle so I should—"

"This is a very special fighting cricket," said Harry. "I got it from my cousin Jim who—"

"Now, now," interrupted Mr. O'Brien. "Give it to me. A cricket is not worth an argument between two friends. Do you boys realize that there are more than two thousand species of crickets?"

"But this one is a champion fighter," Harry said. "He's my good-luck charm from Hong Kong."

Mr. O'Brien looked a little confused at that. He stared down at the cricket in the bottle.

"Gee," said Eddie, "he's only an old pest. When Mr. Swanson gets him, he'll stick him up on his specimen board."

Mr. O'Brien handed the bottle back to Eddie, but Harry tried to grab it back again. "It's mine," he cried.

"All right," said Mr. O'Brien. "I'll tell you what we'll do to settle this argument. Whoever can give me the biological Latin name for this insect may have the privilege of offering him to Mr. Swanson."

Eddie said nothing.

"That cricket's name is Mr. Chang," said Harry. "It's not Latin at all. I told you it's Chinese, and my cousin Jim who's in the Navy was here and he—"

"Very well," said Mr. O'Brien, interrupting Harry. "Neither of you knows the correct answer. The Latin name of this species is *Acheta assimilis*. So both of you may follow me while I carry the cricket to the science lab."

At the lab door, Mr. O'Brien called to Mr. Swanson. "Here's an insect specimen and two eager young contributing scientists."

After Mr. Swanson took the bottle the principal left.

Again Harry tried to explain. "That's mine. He's a fighting champion and he lived in Hong Kong before he came here. Could I please have him back?"

"Is that so?" said Mr. Swanson. "Let me take a good look at him under this magnifying glass."

After he studied the insect, Mr. Swanson looked up at Harry with a smile. "So you say he's a fighting champ from China?"

"Oh, yes," said Harry. "My cousin Jim brought him and—"

"Everybody in our whole room saw Harry catch that cricket," explained Eddie. "Miss Olson won't let us keep bugs in our desks because one time Freddie Melnor dropped a bee down Mary's neck and—"

"I hope Harry won't get into such bad trouble," said Mr. Swanson, not bothering to hear Eddie's complete tale. "However, I really wish you boys would try to find me a *Gryllidae*. That's a pale-green cricket, related to the grasshopper."

"Okay, but this one's mine," said Harry with relief. "So I'd like him back."

"But Miss Olson said he had to give it to you," Eddie insisted.

"I'll tell you what we'll do," said Mr. Swanson. "I'll just keep this cricket anyway. That should settle the argument."

Harry gave Eddie the kind of look that should have turned him into dust. But it didn't.

"Go back to your classroom now, boys," said Mr. Swanson. "But keep looking for a *Gryllidae* if you really want to help us with our project."

4
QUICK RECOVERY

When they left the science lab, Harry felt a sudden urge to knock Eddie down. But what was the use of beating up Eddie? It couldn't bring Mr. Chang back. So he followed Eddie into their room and sat down in misery in his lonely back seat. Without Mr. Chang, it would be all bad luck again.

Lunchtime came, but Harry wasn't hungry. He sat still while everyone else scrambled past him, bumping him and stepping on his toes while they hunted for their coats.

Miss Olson walked down the aisle and asked, "Are you sick, Harry?"

Harry managed to nod his aching head. "Sort of," he agreed.

"Then you'd better not go to the cafeteria with the class," she said. "Sit here and stay quiet. I have to go to the office to see about something. If you're still feeling sick when I come back, I'll call your mother."

Harry managed to keep back the tears. When the room emptied, he felt worse. He opened his lunch box to take out a sandwich, but he looked at it for a long while without taking a taste. For the first time in his whole life, he didn't think he could swallow a bite of his favorite peanut butter and jelly sandwich.

"I wish I could find just one good friend in this whole school of meanies," he muttered.

Then he remembered his hand-painted cricket cage on the ledge outside. At least he'd have that as a souvenir from his cousin Jim. How could Mr. Chang have gotten out of that cage? He was sure he'd put the lid on tight.

Harry stretched his arm out the open window and brought in the cage. The lid was still on. In fact, it was on so tight that he had to use the metal edge of his ruler to pry it off. When he looked inside, he let out a gasp of surprise and relief. There in front of his very own eyes sat his fighting champion, Mr. Chang, as alive as could be and all in one piece.

Harry sat down at his desk, put the cricket in front of him and examined his pet. Then he popped Mr. Chang back in the cage and did a kind of dance around the room. Now he could understand the why and wherefore of this morning's tragedy. Probably Mr. Chang had rubbed his wings together, making happy music as he sat in his outside corner. Some lady cricket in the field beyond, with her knee-joint sound receivers, had heard Mr. Chang's serenade and had come closer. It must have been this lady cricket that Harry had caught. No wonder Mr. Swanson didn't believe him when he said the cricket in Eddie's pill bottle was an undefeated champion fighter from Hong Kong. It was really only an ordinary American female field insect.

Harry was still jumping for joy when Miss Olson walked in. She was glad that he was feeling better.

"If you haven't eaten lunch yet, I have a

very good idea," she said. "A new student is joining our class. His name is Dan Zilmer, so he'll be sitting in back of you. We'll just push your desk forward, since there's room, and put Dan's desk here. He brought his lunch, but the others are ready to leave the cafeteria. Why don't the two of you eat here together and get acquainted?"

Harry was about to say no from habit. However, he glanced up and saw the principal at the door with a tall, skinny, shaggy-haired boy, who looked as lost as Harry had felt his first day here.

"We'll have a desk brought in for Dan right away," said Mr. O'Brien. "Do you have all the textbooks he'll need?"

Miss Olson said she did, and Mr. O'Brien left. Then Harry remembered that he'd made a wish, not long before this new boy appeared, asking for a good friend. Maybe Mr. Chang, who'd been sitting outside on the ledge, had quickly made it come true. So Harry grinned at the new boy named Dan, and the new boy grinned back at him.

"I'm glad you'll be sitting behind me," Harry said. "I never thought there'd be anybody who could have a last name farther back in the alphabet than Weaver."

"You two have a good visit together," said Miss Olson.

"I'll show Dan where everything's kept," offered Harry.

Miss Olson looked surprised. "That's very thoughtful, Harry," she said. "I'm sure you know how it feels to be the new boy."

As soon as Miss Olson left, Harry picked up his sandwich and told Dan, "I'm sure starved. But right before you got here, I didn't feel like eating anything."

"I don't feel so hungry myself," said Dan. "Maybe I'm excited. My dad brought me and we had to wait in the principal's office for a long time. Then we had to answer a lot of questions and wait for the teacher." A worry frown changed Dan's face. "Maybe I won't do so well in this school. I missed a lot while we were getting ready to move. I come from a small school in a small town."

"I'll help you catch up with what you've missed," Harry offered. "I went to a big school before I came here. It was a good one."

"Isn't this a good school?" asked Dan, and he looked so worried that Harry mustered up some enthusiasm to cheer him.

"I guess this is about the best school you could find anywhere around," said Harry. "We've got a science laboratory with an ant farm, all kinds of insects stuck up on a card, and a marching band for music."

Dan looked more interested. "We never had things like that in the little school where I come from," he said.

"The science lab is really for the big junior-high kids," added Harry. "But our science class goes up there for special pictures and demonstrations. We can borrow the science equipment for our experiments and we can take part in some of their study projects if we want to. And we can try out for beginners' band. The teacher asked me to try out, but I haven't yet."

Now Harry had to stop for a breath, and

Dan said, "I'd sure like to beat the drums in a school band."

"Not me," said Harry. "I'm going to play slide trombone."

Harry surprised himself with this decision. Just last week when Miss Olson asked him if he had any interest in music, he said he didn't. He said band music gave him an earache because it was so loud.

Next, Harry showed Dan around the room, praising things he'd paid no attention to before. He showed him how the pencil sharpener worked and took out the textbooks and let Dan copy down his daily schedule. He told about the school library and indicated the shelves of library books loaned to their room for two weeks for free-reading period.

All this impressed Dan so much that Harry was also getting impressed. Dan took a book from the shelf and leafed through it, looking at the pictures. "I'm going to read this one about sailing ships."

"I like steamships better," said Harry.

Right away Dan spotted another book.

"Then here's something for you! Here's something about the Great Lakes steamers."

Harry didn't tell Dan that he'd never before found a book he wanted to borrow from these shelves. The reason was that Mary Marshall was room librarian, and he didn't want to have to go to her to have his book stamped. So he never took a book longer than for the one reading period, which meant he'd never finished reading any of them.

"If some of the kids in our room tease you about anything, just pretend you don't hear them," advised Harry, wishing he'd been able to follow that advice. But now he stood ready to defend his new friend from having the kind of hurtful experiences that he'd had. Dan had lots of things he could get teased about—his pointed chin like a Christmastime elf, his straight brown hair that was too scraggly, and the hole in the elbow of his sweater.

Dan shrugged off this advice. "What do I care what they say?" he told Harry. "When my brother, Bobby, calls me names and I get mad, my dad says words can't break a bone or cause a cut."

About this time Harry made a wish, without realizing his magic cricket was right there. "I sure wish you'd take the same bus I do," he said.

Dan fumbled in his pocket for a slip of paper. "The principal wrote down what bus I'd be taking. I think it's Bus Two."

"It is!" shrieked Harry. "That's the very same bus I take. Your mom and dad must have bought a new house out in Green Hill Acres where I live."

Dan shook his head. "We rent the house we live in and it isn't new. It's the oldest house in the world. At first I thought it must be haunted by ghosts."

"Where is it?" asked Harry. "I haven't seen any old haunted houses around."

"It's a long ways from here," Dan explained. "The principal said Bobby and I would have a long walk from the last bus stop. My dad thought maybe we wouldn't even be in this school district. The house used to be a farmhouse but it's been vacant for a long time. It needs a lot of repairs, but the rent's cheap. My dad has to fix the place up himself."

Dan couldn't tell anything more about his faraway haunted house. The classroom began to fill with chattering classmates just in from a rough-and-tumble session on the playground.

Then two junior-high boys came in carrying a desk. "Where's this go?" one of them asked.

Harry pointed to the place and helped to shove his own desk forward. When Dan was occupying his new place, Harry turned around to say, "Guess why you got to move here and be my new friend?"

Dan whispered back, "Because my dad lost his job in that town where we lived before. He found another one here."

"No, it's because of Mr. Chang," said Harry. "He makes all my wishes come true, and I wished hard today for a friend."

The teacher was asking for immediate quiet, so Harry couldn't make it clear about Mr. Chang just then. However, he became even more happy when Miss Olson said, "Only two students in this class may talk together during the next study period. I'm asking Harry Weaver to help our new boy, Dan Zilmer, if he has any questions."

Eddie Beckman turned around, looked at them, and then complained, "How come Harry gets to help somebody? He never knows the assignments himself, so how can he explain anything to somebody new?"

Miss Olson's answer to Eddie was a sharp "That's enough from you."

Harry was pleased enough at this to make him want to clap his hands in applause. Instead, he just made a face at Eddie.

Let him tattletale to the teacher all he wants to from now on, thought Harry with deep-down satisfaction. Why should I care? Mr. Chang just brought me a friend.

5
MR. CHANG
KEEPS BUSY

Dan Zilmer was fascinated by the fierce black face of the fighter cricket when Harry introduced them to each other after school that day. They were waiting for Bus Two, but they kept their distance from the groups of hopscotch-playing girls and football-kicking boys.

"Let's be careful so Mary Marshall can't see what I've got here," said Harry. "She's got four eyes in the front of her head and they can all see upside down and backward."

Dan said he knew just what Harry meant because his brother, Bobby, was like that. Bobby would come to first grade soon, so Harry would see for himself.

"Bobby couldn't start to school with me today," said Dan. "He caught a bad cold when we were moving. Besides him, I've got younger twin sisters. Watching them's like keeping tabs on two wild bees that have just come out of a broken beehive."

Dan's worry was showing all over his face, even though he'd just been introduced to Harry's new magic maker.

"What if I'm not allowed to stay in your homeroom?" asked Dan. "When I take the tests I'll flunk and get put back. I missed a lot when my mom was sick. I had to stay home to watch the twins for her. We didn't have your kind of new math in our last school. Miss Olson said I couldn't ask my mom and dad for help either, because they didn't have that kind of arithmetic when they went to school."

"You've just got to stay in my room," Harry insisted. "Tomorrow you've got to make Miss Olson think you're a big eager beaver like Eddie. Do an extra credit report for social studies."

"How?" asked Dan.

"It's easy," said Harry, who had never done one. "I could give as many reports as that Eddie and Mary if I wanted to. But I wouldn't ever want to be such a big-mouth know-it-all."

"I couldn't ever be a know-it-all," Dan said. "Today I don't know anything."

"Okay," said Harry, "but you will."

That's why Harry liked Dan so much already. They both had troubles to share. He had advice for Dan and gave it promptly and frankly. "Tomorrow you wave your hand like mad until the teacher calls on you. Then tell any little old thing you know about South Dakota. That's the state we're on in social studies."

"I don't know anything to tell," Dan persisted.

"Read something about it in some book you've got at home," said Harry.

"I don't have anything at home to read," Dan said. "We've got some books but I don't know what's in them. Anyhow, all that stuff is still packed in our moving boxes. My dad's been too busy painting and fixing up to uncrate anything, except what we had to have for eating and sleeping."

By this time the bus came along and everyone rushed to get in. Dan and Harry managed to get a seat together, so the trip home was the shortest Harry had ever made. He would have missed his stop, except that the driver called out, "Hey, Weaver! Don't you get off here, too?"

Harry jumped up. Then, as he started to get off, he changed his mind and asked the driver if he could stay on the bus and ride with his friend to the end of the line.

"Nope," said the driver. "You get off here. Everybody gets off at his regular stop unless he's got written permission from the principal. I've got to go by this list he gives me."

Harry got off reluctantly. He waved to Dan as the bus rolled on its way. Then he trudged up the muddy, rutted road which led to his house, feeling lost and lonely again. In his yard one skinny tree had gray protecting paper wrapped around its two-inch trunk. One dry leaf clung to the longest of the six little twigs that were its branches. He wanted to see the big old tumbledown house where Dan lived and perhaps meet up with a ghost in the attic or cellar.

Dan had given him something to look forward to. "We've got big trees in our yard," he'd said. "Maybe in the summer we can build a tree house."

With all these plans ahead, Harry couldn't let anything happen to Dan, like letting him get put back a grade because he couldn't keep up.

Harry was glad his mother was home. She was in their new pink and white kitchen, mixing piecrust for his favorite apple pie. Right away he poured out the news about the coming of a friend in the person of Dan Zilmer. Several times his mother tried to interrupt, but Harry couldn't stop telling the harrowing tale of Mr. Chang's experience.

"Why did you take that cricket to school?" his mother asked, in a tone that told him he deserved what he'd gotten.

"I'll never take him again," said Harry.

"Now I know why Jim would rather leave him here than take him traveling. If the Chinese have good luck when their crickets stay on their hearths, so should I, although we don't have a hearth in this house."

His mother told him to take Mr. Chang into his room before the cricket crawled into her apple pie, so Harry took him away and put him in the shoe box which he'd found as a place of exercise for Mr. Chang. Then he looked over the set of encyclopedia books his grandmother had given him for his last birthday, and took out the S book. He hurried into the kitchen again to ask his mother if he could take it to Dan so he could find something in it for a report on South Dakota.

"You may not," said his mother. "Dan's house is much too far away if it's almost out of this school district. Furthermore, you said his brother has a cold and I don't want you to catch it."

"But what if Dan flunks?" cried Harry. "The teacher's expecting me to help him."

His mother frowned and shook her head

in exasperation. "Sit down," she ordered, "and listen to me. You should be more concerned about a boy named Harry Weaver. Dan Zilmer sounds like a boy who's well able to take care of himself—but are you? I had a talk with your teacher."

"What'd she say?" Harry asked, but he really didn't want to hear. He knew it couldn't be too good, so he had his excuses ready. "I told you about the mean kids in my room like that Eddie Beckman. Look at all the trouble he made for me today."

"Does Eddie Beckman make you daydream and stare out of the window?" his mother asked. "Does he keep you from taking part in the classwork and getting interested in the activities?"

"I don't like the kids in my room," Harry said.

"Have you ever tried to get to know them?" his mother asked, but Harry shrugged off that question. He'd never thought about it because he didn't care, he told himself often.

Harry listened until his mother finished

scolding him for what the teacher had told her was his "poor attitude." Then he took the S book back to his room where he could stay in the magical presence of Mr. Chang and wish somehow that his teacher could change her attitude about him. Then, all of a sudden he got a better idea for helping Dan. He could read the article on South Dakota himself and copy down some facts so Dan could read them off in class for his report.

He leafed through the book until he came to the page he wanted. Next to the picture of four giant heads staring out from the rocky side of a mountain, it said, "South Dakota, the Sunshine State."

Harry kept reading because he wanted to know what the big heads were all about. A couple of paragraphs down the page, it said, "Located in the central part of the Black Hills of South Dakota is the Mount Rushmore National Memorial, sometimes called the Shrine of Democracy. Here the heads of Washington, Lincoln, Jefferson, and Theodore Roosevelt are carved in granite, the work of the sculptor

Gutzon Borglum. The sculptured heads are so large that Lincoln's nose is longer than the entire face of the sphinx in Egypt."

The faces fascinated Harry. He studied the four stiff and stern Presidents glaring from their rocky perch and wondered what it would be like to come roaming along that road all alone some dark night, with maybe the moonlight shining on them.

"Boy! Oh, boy!" said Harry to himself with a shiver. "You'd think they were going to grab you."

If he ever went there, Harry decided, he'd go in the daylight, and then he'd look up at them and wonder what they were thinking about. Would they think the country was better than it was when they were alive?

Farther down the page he read about a lead plate buried in South Dakota two hundred years ago by two French trappers. In 1913 some schoolchildren had found the plate.

Wouldn't it be great if Dan could dig up something famous like that in the yard of his old haunted house, Harry thought. He'd sure get some extra credit for a special find like that.

Mr. Weaver came home from work by the time Harry was copying down all that it said about the Black Hills gold rush, and about a gold vein found near a town called Lead.

"Your mother is wondering what you're up to in here," his dad told him. "She says you've been quiet for too long a time. But she'll be glad to see you're making use of your books."

"I'm not really reading all this for myself," Harry explained. "It's for a new boy in my room named Dan Zilmer." Then he told his Dad about the powers of the cricket and his need to help his new friend.

"Maybe Mr. Chang will bring us all some good luck," said Mr. Weaver. He sounded as though he couldn't completely believe it but wished it were true.

Again the next morning, Harry gave himself plenty of time to catch the school bus. He wanted to get a seat next to Dan and hand over his collection of facts on South Dakota's history. However, Dan's little brother was sitting with him.

Bobby Zilmer had a thick yellow scarf tied up around his chin and a red cap that covered his ears and hung half over his eyes. He pushed up the cap with his green mittens and grinned at Harry when Dan said, "Here's Harry Weaver. He's in my room."

Right away, Bobby yelled out, "Do you have a lucky cricket in your lunch box?"

This brought a giggle from the girls across the aisle, so Harry sank into a vacant seat behind them. "Not today," he told Bobby in a low voice.

"Why not?" Bobby persisted. "Dan said you did yesterday."

"I've got sandwiches in my lunch box now," said Harry softly, wishing Bobby would turn around and keep quiet. He didn't try to talk to Dan.

When they got off the bus, Dan explained. "Bobby's crazy about all kinds of bugs. Once, when we had cockroaches in our kitchen, my mother found out that it was Bobby who was bringing them in a jar so he could feed them. Some got loose and we had a terrible time getting rid of them."

That morning Dan couldn't walk with Harry to their classroom. He had to take Bobby to the office and get him enrolled. Dan came in while they were pledging allegiance to the flag, so he had to stand up front until they were finished. As soon as Dan sat down, Harry whispered, "Wait till you see what I've got to help you!"

Miss Olson gave him a frowning glance and said, "Now please pay attention." She said she was going to explain some new math problems.

After she'd worked three or four examples on the board, Dan punched Harry on the back and whispered, "I don't get it. Do you?"

"Sort of," Harry whispered back.

Again Miss Olson noticed and asked, "Are you boys paying attention?" Because Harry shook his head yes so vigorously, she told him, "Then come up here to the board and work the next problem for the class."

Harry felt all feet and dangling arms when he walked to the board. However, he forgot the roomful of watching eyes because he wanted to work the problem through and explain it so Dan could understand.

"That's very good," said Miss Olson. "You do understand this very well. I'm glad you were listening to my explanation."

When Harry got back to his seat, Dan mumbled, "Help me some more with these, will you?"

"Sure," said Harry, "as soon as I can get a chance."

The notes on South Dakota had stayed forgotten in Harry's notebook until social studies class. Then he passed them back to Dan and told him, "Here. Just hold up your hand and then read off this stuff when the teacher says you can give your report."

Dan took the notes. When Miss Olson asked if there were any special extra reports, it was Mary Marshall who held up her hand. She gave hers, and then Eddie Beckman asked if he could pass around some picture postcards his aunt had sent him from a trip she'd made to Pierre, the capital of South Dakota.

Harry looked back and asked anxiously,

"How come you aren't waving your hand like I told you? Maybe she'll call on you next."

Dan pointed to Harry's notes spread out in front of him. He was squinting. "What's this say here—and here—and here? Gee, I can't read your writing."

While Harry was turned around, trying to help him make out his scribble, Miss Olson called to them, "Are you boys having trouble? Do you have a question, Dan?"

"No, ma'am," said Dan. He started to stutter with embarrassment. "Harry was trying to help me. And he's got this report."

"I didn't know you had a report, Harry," said Miss Olson, with considerable surprise. "Let's hear what you have to tell us."

Harry was as surprised as Miss Olson.

"You've got to read this stuff yourself," whispered Dan. "Go ahead. I can't."

When Harry was finished, Miss Olson smiled her approval. She marked something in her grade book and said, "That was very interesting, Harry. I'm happy to have you make such a good contribution."

The day that started so fine and dandy for Harry kept on being that way. What wonders would Mr. Chang keep blowing his way, even when he wasn't especially wishing for these things? When school was over, Harry—filled with the highest of hopes—went with Dan to the first-grade room to pick up Bobby.

"Just about anything might happen from now on," Harry said. "Can you imagine me getting elected captain of the fourth-grade basketball team! I didn't even tell Mr. Chang I wanted to be."

However, Dan wanted to put credit where it was due. "That was because I nominated you," he reminded Harry. "Besides, all the other kids who got nominated had already had one turn at being captain."

Bobby paid no attention to Dan's explanation and added his complete belief in Mr. Chang's powers. "I sure wish I could borrow him," said Bobby. "We've got a real fireplace with a hearth in our house. He'd sure like sitting there, I'll bet."

Dan told Bobby to quit asking Harry for

his property. So it wasn't until the next Saturday that Harry realized just how much both Dan and Bobby really needed the help of Mr. Chang.

6

BORROWER AND LENDER

Harry woke up on Saturday morning, surprised that he could feel so sorry for himself because he didn't have to go to school. By the time his mother called him to breakfast, he had his reason ready for having to visit Dan.

"I have to help him do his arithmetic so he won't flunk the test next week. He never had to do sets before and he doesn't know the new-math way to do his division problems."

"You'd better call him first," advised Mrs. Weaver. "He might have other work to do."

"They don't have a telephone yet," said Harry. "I'll just go over and see."

"I'm glad to know you're so anxious to do schoolwork," said Mrs. Weaver. "Dad and I will take you to Dan's house on our way to do the grocery shopping. If he's busy, you can come along with us."

But later that morning, they were unable to find the Zilmers' place. They tried to follow the map that Dan had drawn for Harry, but no place looked anything like the house he had described. Dan had said, "It's a big old gray farmhouse with a sagging front porch, a busted window, and no steps because they've rotted away, and it's at the end of a dirt road that makes two turns before you get to our place."

Harry was afraid his dad would get disgusted and give up, especially when they came to the end of a no-outlet road and found themselves at a cemetery. When they tried to back out, the car slipped sideways into a ditch. Harry consoled Mr. Weaver with the reminder, "We won't have to get a tow truck to lift us out. I've got Mr. Chang along. He'll work his magic for us. I brought him because

Dan's brother has been pestering to see him."

Mr. Weaver managed to get the car out of the ditch, but he refused to give Mr. Chang the credit. And when they did find Dan's house, Mr. Weaver said, "I think the man at the gas station helped more than Mr. Chang. He gave me clearer directions than Dan's map did."

Bobby was out in front playing with a cat as they turned into the driveway of the old house. When he saw them, he waved both arms and jumped up and down. Then he ran to the front door, screaming, "Dan! Guess who's here! Come on out!" In the next breath he asked Harry, "Did you bring your champion cricket with you?"

Dan came out and said he sure did need help with his arithmetic, so Mr. and Mrs. Weaver dropped Harry off and drove away.

Bobby's eyes were an inch from the cricket cage when Harry pried off the lid and boasted, "It isn't everyone who gets such a close look at a prize-winning champ who's earned thousands of dollars in Hong Kong."

"I can tell he's a winner," said Bobby with

awe. When Dan asked him how he could be so sure, he said, " 'Cause he's alive. Like you told me, when a fighting cricket loses a battle, he's dead."

Bobby kept staring at the cricket and exclaiming ecstatically, "Gee, but he's sure beautiful. He's got a black shining coat of armor, just like you said he had, and I can tell he's packed full of ancestors' spirits."

"He sure is," agreed Harry. "See how he's looking around, waving his antennae. He's just itching for a fight to the finish this very second."

"I'll bet he is," Bobby said. "He must get tired of sitting in a sissy painted cage all day listening to someone's wishes."

Bobby started to feel so sorry for the champ that he suggested they let him sit on a real fireplace hearth while he was in their house. "We'll take him into our living room," he offered. "Dad hasn't patched the cracked wall yet and he hasn't painted and papered, so we aren't ready to use it. There's just some chairs and packing boxes sitting around in there."

"Mr. Chang won't mind," said Harry. "He's been to lots of places where they don't have wallpaper, I'll bet."

Dan explained. "My dad can only do work in the house on his day off. He's off today but he had to take my mother to the doctor. So I'm watching the twins. We'd better go inside now and see what they're up to."

Dan led the way into an oversized, freshly painted yellow kitchen. "Dad's got this all fixed up already," he said.

Two chubby honey-haired look-alike little girls, even to the same jelly stains on their chins, were on the floor playing with a dollhouse. They looked up at Harry and grinned.

"Here are the twins, Marietta and Martha," said Dan. "But we call them Mary and Marty."

"Which one's which?" asked Harry, as he looked from one to the other. "How can you tell them apart?"

"I get them mixed up," said Dan. "But my mom doesn't. Come on and I'll show you the rest of the house and then you'll see for yourself why I say it's haunted. I hear the funniest noises at night, like someone walking around and moaning in the attic."

There were long crooked lines and splashes of white marking up the dirt-smudged walls in the dining room. Dan said, "We can sit at this table to do our arithmetic. Dad's done a lot of plaster patching in here, but he doesn't have the furnace working good enough yet, so Bobby can keep the twins in the kitchen where the floor's warmer."

"I won't get cold," said Harry. "I'm still hot from helping to push our car out of that ditch."

Bobby insisted that Harry go on through the hall to see the living room. "You can let Mr. Chang sit on the hearth," he said. "I'll get a piece of lettuce and squash it for him so he won't get hungry."

The twins were following so close on Harry's heels that he stepped back on one pair of toes.

"Did I hurt you?" he asked, but as he bent over to see, one twin made a grab for the cricket cage. "Give Marty dish," she said.

"It's not a dish," scolded Dan. "You keep your hands off. That's a no-no. Go play with your dollhouse."

However, both twins stayed. Now four hands were stretching and pulling on Harry's arm. He held the cage close enough for them to get a brief glimpse and then pulled back. "Go play now," he said. "Do what Dan told you."

Harry was glad to put the cage up high on the mantel shelf. Then Dan said, "Okay, let's get out of here. Mom says we have to keep out until the stuff is unpacked."

Bobby decided to put on his coat again and go back outside. The twins ran to their dollhouse, insisting that Harry come see it before he studied his arithmetic. So Dan had all his school books piled on the table and was waiting when Harry came to help him with their homework.

Then Harry had to explain one page three times and had to turn back to review some other things. "I never had problems like these," said Dan. "I wish I'd been in this school last year."

After they'd filled up sheets of paper with mistakes and corrections, they were interrupted by the sounds of a car stopping and of banging doors, followed by squeals from the twins.

"Mummy's home! Daddy's home!" they chanted as they slapped their hands against the window.

When the Zilmers came in, Dan introduced his friend to them. Mrs. Zilmer smiled at Harry and said pleasantly, "So this is the Harry we've heard so much about. I'm glad you came to help Dan. He needs a friend right now."

"So do I," said Harry.

Dan had told him that moving and fixing up this old house had worn out his mother, but Harry wondered how it could have made her so pale and so thin. His own mother said she could never lose a pound no matter what she did.

Mrs. Zilmer sank into a chair with a sigh and stayed there resting for awhile before she took off her coat. There were dark circles under her eyes and her honey-colored hair hung in straggles, as though she hadn't bothered to comb it.

Harry hoped that his mother could meet

Mrs. Zilmer real soon so she'd see what being thin looked like. Maybe then she'd quit going on diets and refusing to bake his favorite cakes because they were so tempting to her to have around.

"Why don't you stay for lunch?" Mrs. Zilmer suggested to Harry. While she sat resting, the twins took turns crawling into her lap until Mr. Zilmer told them to let her rest.

"My mother told me not to bother you," said Harry.

"He's no bother, is he, Mom?" protested Dan. Then he told Harry. "Gee whiz, you've explained about a million times those problems that I couldn't understand."

"Then you both must be very hungry for some milk and sandwiches," Mrs. Zilmer said. She stood up and put on an apron.

"I'm hungry, too," called Bobby. He had come inside when his mother got home, but now he couldn't decide whether to stay in or go out again. By this time his dad had changed into his work clothes and now he came back into the kitchen with a toolbox.

"Can you put the rope swing in the tree like you promised? " Bobby asked him.

"I've got a long list of things I've promised all of you," said Mr. Zilmer wearily. "But I have only two hands, so give me a chance."

Dan and Harry went back to their homework, and they shut the door between the dining room and kitchen so they wouldn't hear Bobby's chattering. But all of a sudden there was such an outburst of crying from Bobby that Dan jumped up and called, "What happened?"

Bobby kept up his loud crying but didn't answer. Then Dan went into the kitchen, asking, "Will you tell me what's wrong?"

Harry listened. He could hear Mrs. Zilmer scolding Bobby now. "Stop it," she said sharply. "You're not helping me any by carrying on like that."

"Why's he carrying on?" said Dan.

"I don't want her to go to that awful hospital." Bobby wailed louder. "And I don't want Aunt Martha to come stay with us either."

"Shame on you for saying such a thing," said Mrs. Zilmer. "I don't know what I'll do if she doesn't come right away. Someone has to stay with the twins and Dan has missed too much school already. Your dad can't stay with them. He just started on his new job."

When Harry heard this bad news, he hurried into the kitchen. By this time Mr. Zilmer was explaining to Dan, "The doctor says your mother must go to the hospital right away. She needs an operation to make her well again."

Bobby's new burst of crying started the twins wailing. They held on to their mother's skirt, repeating Bobby's words, "Don't go. Don't go."

Mrs. Zilmer gave Bobby a hard shake. "Now look what you've done," she said. "You've gotten everyone excited."

Bobby opened the back door and rushed out without his coat. His mother took it from the closet and pushed it at Dan. "Go take this to him," she said. "I can't have him sick with another cold at a time like this."

"Maybe I'd better not stay for lunch," said Harry, reaching for his coat.

"But it's almost ready," said Mrs. Zilmer. "I'm sorry that Bobby frightened everyone. I had no idea he'd get so upset when I told him."

Harry went outside too. Dan had given the coat to his brother. Bobby jammed his arms into the sleeves, crying, "I don't want her to go. She'll never come back from that terrible hospital. My friend Ricky's mom went to the hospital. They told Ricky it would make her better but it didn't."

"She'll get better," said Harry. He tried to think of something to help Bobby. "My grandma is fine and she's been to the hospital three times."

That didn't help. Bobby started crying again. Then Harry thought of something that he knew would make both boys feel better. "I'll tell you what I'll do," he said. "I know how to make sure your mom *will* come back from that operation all better. I'll leave Mr. Chang sitting right where he is in his cage on your hearth."

Bobby's wet face brightened. "Will you? Oh, will you let him stay to bring us luck?"

"I said I would—didn't I?" said Harry generously.

Bobby was full of promises. "If you let Mr. Chang stay, I'll look until I find some red ants and some mosquitoes too, even lotus seeds, everything he used to like to eat when he lived back in Hong Kong."

Dan had some misgivings about the whole thing. "How would you get along without him, Harry?" he asked. "Anyhow I might forget to feed him because I'll have a lot to do helping to take care of the twins."

"Why would *you* have to feed him?" Bobby asked his brother angrily. "You're not the only one that does things around here, even if Mom thinks you are."

"All right," said Harry. "I didn't mean to start a big argument. But you leave him sitting where he is. Reach up and put the food in his cage. And as soon as you know your mother's operation is over okay, I'll take him home."

Bobby's grief was over when he went in again. Harry had a few worrisome moments about leaving Mr. Chang, but it was too late to back out now. He was finishing up his last bite of lunch when he heard his dad's car. "I've got to go," he said. "They're here for me."

Harry grabbed up his coat, thanked Mrs. Zilmer for the lunch, and ran out. Outside, he was met by his mother who had gotten out of the car, saying she wanted to meet Dan's parents, if it was all right with them.

For the next few minutes, they all stood inside and introduced each other and talked. When Harry told his mother about Mrs. Zilmer's expected hospital visit, his mother said, "Everything will go fine, I'm sure. If there's anything I can do, let me know."

As soon as they were on their way, Harry said, "I'm helping them an awful lot. I've loaned them Mr. Chang to sit on their parlor mantel, but I hope he doesn't forget me."

"That was generous," said Mrs. Weaver, "especially since you seem to think you need the good luck he's been bringing your way."

7

DOUBLE WORK LOAD

The next Monday morning, Bobby Zilmer was sitting alone on the bus. When Harry got on, he boasted, "Today I didn't tell my mom not to go to the hospital and I didn't cry when she went."

"Did you feed Mr. Chang?" asked Harry.

"I fed him something better than he ever ate before, I'll bet you," said Bobby. "I found some fat water bugs in our cellar near our leaking water pipe. I caught some in a jar and then I put in some spinach left over from my supper."

Harry frowned. "I didn't tell you he'd like water bugs, did I?"

"No," said Bobby. "But you didn't tell me he wouldn't like them."

"You're supposed to give fighting crickets boiled chestnuts and lotus seeds," said Harry. "In Hong Kong, if they get a stomachache from eating too much, their owners feed them red ants. If they catch cold, they're supposed to get chopped mosquitoes."

"I looked for those things because you told me that already," said Bobby. "Do you suppose Mr. Chang will get mad and bring me bad luck because I fed him water bugs?"

"He's not mad at you," said Harry, although he wasn't sure. But he felt that Bobby had enough to worry about without his adding any more. "Look at the miracles he made happen to me and all I've been feeding him is hamburger and squashed-up lettuce."

During the first few minutes of the school day, Harry thought his good luck had gone with the visiting Mr. Chang. Dan's back seat was empty, so he felt as lonely as ever. Then, when Eddie Beckman came by to hang up his coat, he stepped on Harry's toe, which made him yell "ouch," and that brought Miss Olson hurrying his way.

Harry had braced himself for a scolding, but the teacher's frown was not because of anything he'd done.

"Can you get Dan Zilmer's assignments to him this week and make sure he understands everything?" she asked. "He's already so far behind and now he has to miss more school until his aunt arrives. His father called this morning and told me about Mrs. Zilmer's poor health."

"I won't let him miss anything," said Harry. "My mom told his mom that she'd drive me over there anytime if he needed help."

"Good," said Miss Olson. "If Dan could keep up with the class at home without help, I could just send the assignments home with his brother."

"You won't need to do that. I'll go over to Dan's house and tell him everything we did in class," said Harry.

This pleased Miss Olson. "You have improved in many ways, Harry," she said. "Did your mother tell you we had a talk?"

"Yes, she did," said Harry. "But that wasn't the reason I've improved."

Harry was about to tell her about his good-luck charm, but Mary Marshall was waving for the teacher's attention.

"Dan Zilmer is absent," reported Mary. "Who will take his place on the keep-the-blackboards-clean committee?"

Again Miss Olson looked at Harry. "Could you be Dan's substitute?" she asked. "I don't know all that he's volunteered to do. Our room chairman can tell you."

Harry had a sinking feeling. Because of his own insistent advice, Dan had volunteered for any job he could get. This would show the teacher, Harry had told him, that "you're awful interested and that you're trying."

While Dan was gone, Harry was too busy to feel sad. He couldn't so much as throw a glance out the window or he might be missing something. What he missed, Dan would miss also. Several times his mother drove him over to see Dan. Every time Bobby bragged about Mr. Chang's contentment.

"He's fatter now than when you brought him," said Bobby. "Maybe smashed water bugs are his favorite dish."

"Maybe," said Harry. "But he looks just the same to me. And don't let him get lost in any of those cracks in the plaster."

"I won't," Bobby always promised.

During the next weekend, Harry couldn't help Dan. Instead, he went with his mother and dad to visit Grandma Weaver who lived near Middletown, Ohio, which was also his cousin Jim's hometown. His grandma told about all the amazing good luck that Jim kept on having. "He's got orders to stay in the states for six months and go to school. He might even get married."

"Why, Mr. Chang did it all!" said Harry, impressed with the fact that when a lucky cricket had started his magic-making, one good thing led to another.

His grandma was puzzled. "Who's Mr.

Chang?" she asked. "The name sounds
Chinese. I don't think I've heard Jim mention
him."

Harry decided not to try to explain to his
grandma about crickets that carried the spirits
of their ancestors. She swatted every insect she
laid her eyes on, so she wouldn't be able to believe they were anything but germ-carrying
pests.

After Harry got back home from Ohio, he
received a message from Dan, delivered by
Bobby on the bus. "He says don't bring any
school assignments or books to him. My Aunt
Martha's coming so he can go back to school."

Several days later, Harry was greeted with
happy news from Bobby. "My mom's okay, so
I've got Mr. Chang and his cage here to give
you. Dan said I had to give Mr. Chang back as
soon as Mom's operation was over, and it's
over."

"I'm awful glad to get him back," said
Harry. "The teacher's giving us a lot of tests
and I'll be needing all the magic I can get."

"He helped us," said Bobby. "So I'm

going to do something real super-special for him. I never did find any lotus seeds, but maybe I can find something else even better."

"Don't bother," said Harry. "Maybe by now he likes American food even better than Chinese. Jim said *he* sure does."

The bus was so noisy that morning that no one could have heard Mr. Chang chirping. When Harry got him to his classroom, he again put him on the ledge outside the window. But this time no lady cricket came in answer to his song. At the end of the day, Mr. Chang returned safely home by way of Harry's pocket.

The next day Dan came back, looking sleepy and still sad.

Harry tried to cheer him. "You don't have to worry about your mom anymore, do you?" said Harry. "I guess Mr. Chang did what we asked him to do."

But Dan was snappy instead of full of gratitude. "Bobby had a nerve asking you to lend us that cricket," he said. "You shouldn't have let him have it."

Harry's feelings were hurt, but he didn't say anything mean to Dan. Dan had been through a worrying time and he had a lot of make-up work to do, even though Harry had knocked himself out helping him. For instance, during English class, Dan let out a groan when Miss Olson reminded the class, "Your English papers are due on Friday, so I hope by now all of you are completing and proofreading your compositions. Your paper is important."

"What paper is she talking about?" whispered Dan. "You never told me about any."

"Sure I did," said Harry, but right away he wondered if he really had. There had been so much to tell Dan. "Didn't I ask you what unforgettable character you know, because that's what this paper's supposed to be about."

"I don't know any character like that," said Dan. "Did you write one?"

"I wrote about George Washington," said Harry. "He's unforgettable because I wrote a paper about him in every grade I've been in school." He opened his notebook and showed

Dan a couple of pages filled front and back with his very largest handwriting.

"I'll never get time to write a long piece like that by Friday," said Dan. "Aunt Martha came, but I have to help her."

Harry opened his notebook and offered, "Here, take mine. Copy it into your handwriting. That won't take you long, and I'll do another one."

Harry thought Dan was too quick to push it away and say, "No. I don't want to do that."

Harry tried to think of some other way to help Dan, who wasn't convinced that George Washington was unforgettable enough for a subject. Dan thought it had to be about someone you had really known well and had talked to.

When Harry was squashing a lettuce leaf for Mr. Chang, he suddenly got his good idea. "I'll write something for Dan about Mr. Chang," he said out loud, snapping his fingers. "Dan won't ever forget him after how he helped his mom."

When he asked his mother if he could use

her typewriter for some important school work, she said, "Go ahead. Learning to type is a good way to learn to spell."

But before Harry could hunt out the letters on the typewriter, a very hard job for him in itself, he had to think up what he could say about his famous cricket. He wrote it all down in pencil first, describing the black, shining good looks of his champion fighter and the importance of these insects in China. His mother came to the bedroom and said, "Are you really doing school work? I've never seen you working so hard at anything all year."

"I sure am," said Harry, "and I've got to hurry and get it all done."

"Then you should have started sooner," said his mother. "That's something else the teacher complained about. She said you're too slow to start your assignments."

Harry didn't take time to defend himself against this charge. He needed his mother's help in finding some typing paper and fixing the margins on her typewriter.

The more Harry thought about Mr.

Chang's ancestors, the more he wondered who they were. If they were characters in history like the ferocious Mongols or the powerful Ming emperors, maybe they'd be written up in his reference book under C for China. Then he took time to read about some of the important historical people.

His mother was curious and impressed enough over his hours of concentrated work to help him put in a few commas and periods and to explain why they were needed.

"This is very good," she told him. "I'm sure your teacher will like this."

"I hope so," said Harry, without adding the fact that Dan's passing or failing in English might depend on his getting this done and done well.

And wouldn't Dan be surprised and relieved when Harry handed him his homework, with nothing more to do than sign his own name across the top.

Sure enough, Dan was surprised, but he wasn't so happy about it. "Gee whiz," he said, "you did all that for me for nothing. I told

Aunt Martha I'd missed that assignment and she helped me think of an unforgettable character. She said I should write about my Uncle Wally and she said she could tell me a lot about him because she's married to him. That way, I wouldn't have to read a lot of stuff in the library."

Harry grabbed up his wasted effort and started to tear up the pages, but Dan stopped him. "Don't do that. Let me read what you wrote."

Harry handed over his composition with a look of disgust and disappointment. And he sat glumly staring out of the bus window.

Dan read to the very end. Then he gave Harry a sharp jab with his elbow. "This is good," he said. "It's a lot better than what you wrote about George Washington, especially because I couldn't make out your handwriting when you showed me that one. But this is neat-o."

"It's a neat-o for the wastebasket," grumbled Harry.

"But why?" cried Dan. "It's your work,

for Pete's sake. Why don't you put your own name on it and turn it in today?"

Harry felt cheated after working so hard, but he decided to take Dan's advice.

8

A REWARD FOR
MR. CHANG

A few days later it was Bobby's turn to have an exciting surprise for Harry. "I'm not going to tell you what it is, not until you bring Mr. Chang back to our house, because it's the extra-special thing I told you I'd find for him."

"Did you find red ants?" said Harry.

"Nope," said Bobby, flashing a satisfied grin. "But you won't find out 'cause it's a secret until you come over."

"I don't know when I can come." Harry hesitated, sensing something amiss in all this eagerness.

"How about early tomorrow?" suggested

Bobby. "It's Saturday, and Mr. Chang's going to get a big thrill, and you, too."

The next morning, Harry asked his mother if he could take his bike and ride over to the Zilmers' place. "But it's not to do school work, so if you need me for something—" he told her, half hoping she'd say he couldn't go.

He was torn between curiosity over Bobby's treat for Mr. Chang and the suspicion that Bobby's glee and secrecy had stirred up.

However, his mother was more than obliging. She urged him to go and have fun. "After all that work you put in writing that English composition, you deserve a day for play, and so does Dan."

When Harry got there—the cage containing Mr. Chang in his pocket—he met Dan's Aunt Martha, a plump, smiling woman with brown eyes and a roll of hair on top of her head. She was hanging up clothes when he pedaled into the yard on his bike. On the other side of the house, Harry was surprised to see a bunch of Bobby's first-grade pals who yelled, "Here he is! Now we can have it."

"Have what?" asked Harry. "And where's Dan?"

"He had to go to the store with my dad," Bobby explained. "But he's not interested in crickets anymore." With this he held up a big jar that had a piece of thin cloth tied over the top. Sitting inside the jar on a tiny twig was a big black cricket who could have passed for Mr. Chang's twin brother.

"Where'd he come from?" asked Harry.

"My dad was digging in the cellar to get to our leaking water pipe. I was helping him, and when I looked down, there was this guy. I named him Mr. Smith, but I'll bet Mr. Chang will beat him when we let them fight."

"Fight!" cried Harry. "Why should they fight?"

" 'Cause isn't that what they're supposed to do if they're fighting crickets?" insisted Bobby.

"But we don't have the right kind of fighting arena," said Harry. "You don't think I'd let you put Mr. Chang in that skinny jar, do you?"

"I've got a good thing for them to fight in," said Bobby. "It's just like what you said your cousin Jim saw them fighting in, in Hong Kong." He took Harry to a wooden box on which he'd placed a low-rimmed flat blue bowl. "They can't hop out of this."

"We'd need a rat whisker," said Harry. "In Hong Kong they've got to tickle their legs with a rat whisker to get them mad enough to fight to the death."

"I remembered that," Bobby cried. "My cat Florabelle is always losing whiskers, so I saved one." He reached into his pocket and brought out a wadded-up Kleenex. "Here it is. How would a cricket know if the whisker that tickled him came from a rat or a cat?"

By this time a couple of Bobby's pals started to complain. "When's the fight going to start?" and "Aw nuts, I came all the way over here and I haven't seen anything," and "How come we can't see this Mr. Chang that makes magic?"

"My cricket is very special," protested Harry. "He wouldn't fight anyone unless he knew it was right. Over in Hong Kong they have an announcer who calls out their names and tells their winning records."

"Okay then," said Bobby. "Here I go. I'm the special announcer. In this bowl before your very own eyes, you see Mr. Smith, cellar cricket from the United States. Beside him is Mr. Chang, lately of Hong Kong."

He interrupted himself to ask Harry, "How many fights has he won?" Then he looked into the blue bowl, saw only one cricket, and complained, "How come you don't put Mr. Chang in there? Are you afraid Mr. Smith will beat him up? I'm not, and I think he's just itching for a fight instead of sitting all day in a sissy cage with painted flowers on it."

Because he could think of nothing else to delay the action, Harry opened the cage and gently lifted out his miracle maker. He placed him in the bowl and was immediately the center of shoving confusion. Feet tramped on feet and elbows bumped complaining heads.

"Get out of my way," yelled one of Bob-

by's smallest pals, and he pushed against Harry's bent back for a closer look. By now, Harry had his eyes fastened on both black crickets, who ogled each other only inches apart. Another push wobbled the wooden box on which the bowl had been placed.

"Watch out," shrieked Harry. "Quit that shoving."

The shoving came harder. The box shook and almost upset. This made the bowl tip and Bobby reached out to grab it. When Harry looked again, he saw only one cricket in the bowl.

"Where's Mr. Chang?" he shrieked.

"Where's Mr. Smith?" yelled Bobby. Then he begged his friends, "Help me look for him. I'll bet he's scared of Mr. Chang and he's hiding somewhere in the grass."

Harry ordered everyone to move both feet and he searched the ground but found no frightened cricket.

"Maybe he ran down a deep hole," guessed Bobby, almost crying with disappointment.

"Maybe it was Mr. Chang who got away," said one of Bobby's friends. "Maybe he's digging his way through the earth to Hong Kong by now."

Everyone laughed at this but Harry. Right away he had grabbed the cricket left alone in the bowl and popped him into the cage. But now he wasn't so sure. Maybe Bobby should have put him back in Mr. Smith's jar.

An auto had driven up close and a horn was honking impatiently.

"That's my mother," said one of Bobby's pals. "I've got to go. But I sure got cheated coming over here and not seeing anything."

"How'd you get cheated?" said Bobby. "I didn't charge you anything to come, did I? Maybe I should have, just to let you *look* at a real fighting cricket like Mr. Chang."

By this time someone else had to go home. Then another first-grader remembered he was due to be taken to the dentist. He got on his bike and rolled on his way fast.

"I think that was Mr. Chang who ran away," said the boy who was left. "He wasn't so brave, even if he was filled up with big-shot ancestors' spirits."

"Aw, go on home," Bobby said. "Mr. Chang brought me a lot of good luck, so he is, too, brave."

While this argument was in progress, Harry turned aside and opened the cage. He gave the occupant a long, searching look. Was this Mr. Chang sitting so quietly content? Or was it Mr. Smith, sitting still because he was surprised to find himself in such a fancy home? How could he ever be sure? Of course, if he started having a fast streak of bad luck, far worse than he'd ever had before, he'd know that Mr. Chang was digging his way to Hong Kong and that he was feeding a common cricket from the Zilmers' leaking cellar. Harry shivered thinking of how bad this kind of bad luck might be.

9
WHO IS WHO?

Harry dreaded the coming of a new school week now that he was puzzled about his lucky charm. Did Mr. Chang have that much hair on his legs? Was he that size or bigger, or maybe smaller? Was he that black-brown color or hadn't he been more black-black?

However, very soon Harry had such a bang-up pile of good luck that he knew Mr. Chang was none other than *himself.*

In the next arithmetic test, the teacher announced, "We had one perfect score. Harry Weaver, you did very well, I must say."

Eddie Beckman cried out, "Then he must have cheated. I could cheat, too, if I got to sit way back there in the corner."

This time Miss Olson told him, "I've had enough of these comments from you, Eddie. I'd better not hear one more, and just so you'll remember you can stay in at recess and write Harry an apology."

The next day, Harry's team won the first basketball play-off in the grade-school tournament. Chuck Moller, the sixth-grade bully on the bus, was referee. At the end of the game he gave Harry a slap on the back and said, "Say, you're okay. Nice fast footwork." Then Dan grinned at him and got everyone else on the team to stand together and yell, "Rah! Rah! Harry!"

"You know why we won," Harry told Dan when gym period was over and they were sitting together on a bench in the locker room. "I wished we would. Mr. Chang's still making wishes come true."

"Aw, nuts!" said Dan. "I was awful good in basketball at the school where I came from. I made a lot of good basket throws in this game. Didn't you notice?"

"How come you don't act as though you

believe in Mr. Chang?" protested Harry. "Do
you know what I read about the Chinese,
when I was doing that English composition
for you about him being so unforgettable?"

"What'd you find out?" grumbled Dan as
though the whole thing bored him.

"Do you know why they never liked for-
eigners to come in and put up railways and
bridges?" asked Harry instead of telling him.

"No, why?" snapped Dan.

" 'Cause they were scared their ancestors'
spirits would be disturbed and they'd have
bad luck. That's why the valleys where their
ancestors' spirits are stay so beautiful. So, of
course, that's where there are lots and lots
of lucky crickets like Mr. Chang. And the
Chinese really do believe in them and all their
good-luck charms," said Harry, shaking a
warning finger at doubting Dan. "Why, before
they ever start anything, they throw down two
pieces of bamboo root. If these pieces turn a
certain way, they know their ancestors are saying *yes* and *go ahead, start*. If they turn the
other way, they're saying *beware* and *don't*.

The look on Dan's face was still disbelief, and annoyance on top of that.

"All right. I'll tell you what," said Harry. "If Mr. Chang makes one more good thing happen to me, then you've just got to believe he's got all those courageous ancestors' spirits."

"I wish you'd talk about something else once in a while," said Dan, and he walked away.

The something good happened to Harry so soon that he was stunned. He was happily swinging his gym bag on his arm, on his way back to his homeroom, when Miss Olson stopped him and said, "I have good news for you, Harry. I liked your English composition so much that I gave it to Mr. Swanson to read. He has invited anyone to make contributions to his study project on the uses of insects."

"I know," said Harry.

"But your composition so impressed Mr. Swanson that he is placing your name on the Junior High Science Honor Roll, and he'd like you to bring Mr. Chang back to school. He wants to meet this fighting champion from Hong Kong."

"I sure will bring him," promised Harry. "I'll bring him tomorrow."

"Fine," said Miss Olson. "I'm sure Mr. Swanson will take very good care of him."

Harry floated back to his room as though little wings had sprouted on his feet. When Dan came hurrying in behind him, Harry asked, "Where've you been?"

Again Dan had a tight-lipped look. "Getting a drink," he said.

Then Harry repeated in a hissing whisper all the praise Miss Olson had heaped on him. "So now, you've got to believe Mr. Chang's a magic wish-maker-come-true. I'm almost afraid to bring something so valuable back to school. I remember that awful day when the lady cricket was here."

"Don't bring him!" cried Dan. "Don't you dare bring that cricket to Mr. Swanson, or he'll just laugh in your face like he did the last time."

"Why would you say a thing like that? " asked Harry, feeling the sting of this last insult. Are you jealous or something because you didn't turn in that paper that I did for you?"

There was no time to say more. Miss Olson was calling the class to order. However, as soon as Harry could talk again, he turned around and told Dan, "I sure wish you'd tell me why you're acting so funny."

What Dan answered back was even more puzzling. "If Mr. Swanson hadn't asked you to bring your cricket to school, I would never have told you. Then you'd just keep on thinking you're lucky."

"Tell me what?" demanded Harry, but the teacher saw him turning around, so at that moment Dan didn't tell him anything more.

When they were together after school, Harry asked the same question.

Now Dan had to answer. "That isn't Mr. Chang you've got home in your cricket cage," he said.

"How would you know?" Harry demanded. "You weren't even there that Saturday when Bobby wanted Mr. Chang to fight Mr. Smith. You were at the store with your dad."

But Dan said he was telling the truth.

"You never even brought Mr. Chang to our place that day. I never told Bobby. I never told anyone because I never wanted you to find out—" Dan looked stricken. His words died away and he twisted his mouth as though it hurt him to talk.

"But I sure did bring Mr. Chang to your house," Harry insisted. "If you'd been there—"

"I didn't want to be there," said Dan. "I knew you couldn't bring Mr. Chang because Mr. Chang was already dead."

"Dead!" cried Harry. "How could he be? How can you stand there and say such a terrible thing?"

"Because it's true," said Dan. "It happened the very first day you brought him to our house. I didn't know Marty could get a chair and reach up to that mantel shelf where we put him. I came in the room to feed him and I caught her with the cage in her hand. I didn't know she'd already pried off the lid when I went to grab the cage away from her. And I didn't know Mr. Chang had fallen out onto the floor, not until I took a step and heard a crunch and then I looked down—"

Dan couldn't go on.

"But who've I got now? Who did I take to your house when Bobby fixed up that cricket fight?"

Dan was telling it all now in his own way and in his own good time. "I would have walked all the way to one of those valleys in Hong Kong if I could have," said Dan. "I'd have done anything to get you another fighter just like him. But I had to hunt down in our cellar. It has an earth floor, and so I dug around a hole in the corner and moved a couple of stones. There I saw a huge bunch of crickets and I picked out the biggest, fattest, and blackest one and I put him in your cricket cage. But Mr. Swanson is smart about insects. He'll know it's not a fighter from Hong Kong, and he'll make fun of you or call you a liar."

Harry turned and ran away from Dan. They had been waiting for the bus, so a guard grabbed Harry and scolded, "Where do you think you're going. It's against the rules to go back into the building once you're out."

There was nothing else to do but climb into the bus. He wouldn't sit near Dan after what he'd done. He stared out the window trying to decide what he'd tell the science teacher about the missing Mr. Chang. Would Mr. Swanson ever believe that once he'd had a lucky cricket from Hong Kong—a famous descendant of the great Genghis Khan?

When Harry got up and made his way to the door of the bus, Dan reached out to him, but Harry jerked away. "Your Mr. Chang *was* a lucky cricket," Dan said. "I always believed he was the luckiest magic maker I ever heard of in my whole life."

Harry gave no answer and jumped off the bus. As soon as he got home, he went to his room and looked at the plain old American cricket that Dan had dug up from his cellar. There was nothing he could do except let him go free to find Mr. Smith or to find himself his own hole-in-the-ground home in Green Acres. Harry's mother found him staring dejectedly at the occupant of the shoe box, trying to make up his mind as to what he should do now.

"Are you doing your school work?" his mother said. But she didn't wait for his answer before she told him, "You are a very lucky boy because your dad and I have decided to take you on a vacation this summer to the Western ranch you've always wanted to see. You can ride a horse and—"

"When?" cried Harry. "When do we start?"

"After school's out," said his mother. "We weren't going to spend much for a vacation trip after the expenses of moving out here, but you deserve a reward for making such an improvement in your school work. Your teacher says you've changed your attitude for the better and improved in everything."

Then his mother turned her head to listen. "Didn't I hear someone knocking at our back door?"

Harry followed behind her when they went to see who it was. There on the back step stood Dan.

"Come in," said Mrs. Weaver. "What a nice surprise!"

"I was on the bus," said Dan, looking at Harry with sad eyes and rows of worry wrinkles on his face. "I got off the bus at the next stop after Harry's, so I'm sure in trouble with the bus driver. He yelled that it wasn't my stop, but I jumped off anyhow and ran here fast, so I could—"

Mrs. Weaver interrupted his breathless explanation with a happy thought. "If you did all that, you must have very important business to discuss with Harry. Why don't you both go into the rumpus room and I'll bring you some milk and cookies."

"That's fine," said Dan. He caught his breath and tried to smile.

When they were alone, he told Harry, "You didn't wait to hear everything I did for Mr. Chang. You told me that when champion crickets die from accidents or old age, their owners honor them with fancy funerals."

"Sure," said Harry, who was fighting back his angry tears again. "But all Mr. Chang got was being stepped on by your big foot."

"But he got more than that," said Dan. "I gave him a fancy funeral. I walked all the way down to that store on the main road, and I got a wooden cigar box with gold paper on it. I found some silver and green ribbon saved from a Christmas present. Then I got a piece of white cloth with fancy work and lace on it, torn from a dress that Marty wore out. I folded this in the box on top of some soft cotton fluff. Then I put Mr. Chang in this fancy coffin and I wrapped it with more ribbon. I buried him in our backyard, and his grave is right near a big lilac bush. I sprinkled some of my mother's zinnia seeds on top, so he'll have some flowers growing on his grave this summer."

"Did you do all that?' said Harry. He blew his nose and his frown disappeared.

"I didn't know any Chinese words," Dan continued. "And I didn't know any wise Confucius sayings, so I just said, 'Rest in peace, Mr. Chang, Famous Champion, and keep your ancestors' spirits working for Harry Weaver so he'll stay lucky all his life.'"

Harry's disappointment eased as he listened to this very proper funeral arranged for Mr. Chang.

"That was nice," he said. "You did the right thing because in Hong Kong, the courageous spirits are passed right on to other crickets hatched from eggs near the champion's grave."

Dan took a deep breath of relief. He stood straight as though he'd just gotten rid of an unbearable burden. "Then you aren't mad at me anymore?"

"Naw," said Harry. "You can't stay mad at your best friend. Besides, my mom says being mad at someone is just something in your mind and you can always change your mind."

There was another feeling Harry was changing right then and there, and fast. All this good luck he'd been having wasn't because of the cricket at all! He'd been making his own good luck, all by himself. So why couldn't he keep right on having more and more of the same?

Mrs. Weaver had brought them a heaping

plate of chocolate-chip cookies, Harry's favorite kind. He remembered his good manners in time to pass the plate to Dan before he took three for himself.

"Maybe it's better it happened this way," said Harry, as they munched on the treat together. "I couldn't have been bothered out West on a real horse ranch with a tiny cricket cage, and there are no kennels for insects like there are for dogs and cats to stay in.

"So I'm still lucky and I can stay that way," Harry decided. But most of all he knew he was lucky because he and Dan were the best of good friends again. And Harry intended to keep it that way, whether they were together or in different homerooms next year.

And in the meantime they had an insect story to tell the science teacher.